I SAW BIGFOOT

BOOK 3

ETHAN HAYES

FREE REIGN

ISBN 13: 978-1-953462-71-8

Free Reign Publishing, LLC
San Diego, CA

FREE REIGN
Publishing

CONTENTS

ONE
NEW YORK SIGHTING

IN THE SUMMER OF 1978, I went on a hiking trip. This year I was in the Wanakena wilderness of New York. I was looking for more of a challenge, so I selected a secluded area of the wilderness. I told my friends I would be hiking for about ten days.

On day one I began to get an unsettling feeling that I was being watched. I was unfamiliar with this area, and I really wasn't going to give up so easily. I attributed that feeling of being watched to a rogue bobcat or a moose. Still, I couldn't shake the feeling of being followed. I continued to hear something rustling in the underbrush and keeping pace with me.

Before it got too late in the day, I found a place to camp for the night. I set up my tent and went down to the river to catch my dinner. To be on the safe side, I had brought along extra food and tied it up in a secure location so animals wouldn't get into it. When I returned to my camping spot later that afternoon, I passed several others who were camping in the area. They were far enough away so they didn't bother me, and I still felt like I was alone in the wilderness. I knew I would be moving further down the trail the next day.

I cooked my dinner and cleaned up the campsite. As I was tying up the last of the remains, I heard what sounded like a scream. It pierced the air and was unlike any animal sound I had ever heard. The howling continued, intermittently, for the next two hours.

After the screaming stopped, I was able to get a great night's sleep. The next morning was nice. I enjoyed the hiking and solitude of nature and spent most of the day exploring the wilderness. It was a long day. I was ready for sleep after dinner and crawled into my sleeping bag shortly after dark. I was only asleep for two or three hours when I heard the howling begin again. It started out as a low snarl or grumble and then quickly twisted into a high pitched and ear-shattering scream. The intensity of the yell was overpowering and a bit frightening. Again, it only lasted a few hours. While I could hear it move around me, it never drew any closer to me.

When I woke the next morning, I found that my campsite had been invaded while I slept. Though I initially suspected raccoons or coyotes, I didn't think much of it at the time. Until I looked up. I found my food bag had been taken down from the tree. It looked like the line had been cut. I thought at first that a bear was responsible, though I couldn't figure out how it would have reached the bag. I then realized I was without my food supply. I knew I would have to live off the land. Even if I turned around and went back now, I still had a two-day hike ahead. There was a stream close, and I could survive on fish for two days until I got back to my truck. While that was not an ideal situation for me, I had survived this way before and I knew I could do it again.

I rolled up my tent and decided to make it the best hike I could. That night, I set up my tent once more, knowing it was only one day back. There I could get more supplies and try again. I went down to the stream to catch my dinner and came back to camp to cook it. This was just a kink in the plan, and I was determined to make the best of it.

I was rather tired from the long day of hiking, so I turned in early, shortly after it got dark. I hadn't been asleep for more than a few hours when I heard what sounded like pebbles hitting the side of my tent. I stepped out, hoping to spot the joker. When I went outside, I was met with a foul odor and a strange silence. The entire forest was still.

Returning to my tent, I hoped for a peaceful rest, but the night had other plans. Again, the ear-piercing screams began again. The screams only lasted for a few minutes that night but was quickly followed by the unnatural silence of the forest. While it was quiet, I was rather unnerved. I rested the best I could until daylight.

When dawn broke, I packed up my belongings and set off. I still had the feeling of being watched. I was determined to make it home before dark, so I walked for hours before stopping. My hunger eventually made me take a break and led me to the river for a quick fish or two.

I wasn't there long before I caught sight of a massive figure out of the corner of my eye. This figure in the woods was unlike any animal I had seen before. It was shuffling through the brush and had paced me through the forest. To startle it away, I stood up and yelled, throwing a rock at the same time. It didn't scare the creature off. It only made it stop and stare directly at me, almost challenging me to do it again. It was a large creature, covered completely in hair and looked almost like a primate. It glared at me for a few seconds and then it turned and walked away, disappearing deeper into the woods.

I decided not to stay any longer than I needed to. I quickly made a small fire and cooked the fish I had caught, then I continued back to the trail. As I got closer to the edge of the wilderness, I noticed that the sounds of the forest gradually returned. By the end of the trail, it was all a memory. I saw my truck in the parking lot and quickly made it to the truck, tossing everything in the cab with me.

I stopped at the ranger's station, and I told the ranger about the events I had just experienced. He chuckled and said that several campers had made reports of Bigfoot sightings in the area.

TWO
ARKANSAS SIGHTING

IN 2013 I was living in Lawrenceville, Arkansas, near a semi-rural area not too far from the Maddox River. It was mid-December, somewhere around 9:30 PM, I had a strange experience. On my property, I had almost an acre of land. Near the back portion of my land there was a tributary that ran off from the Maddox River. There were several greenbelts that connected and ran through the community. My house was at the end of the road on a cul-de-sac and was bordered by a densely wooded region.

As I returned home that night from a holiday shopping trip, I noticed an unusual figure standing near the tree line. The house next door was vacant at the time, so I kept an eye out for anything unusual on the cul-de-sac. The figure was about 60 yards away from me. When I pulled into my drive and headed towards the garage, my car's headlights passed over the figure, lighting it up for a moment. The figure appeared to be an extremely tall, upright creature covered in hair. It had its back turned to my car. When the headlights hit it, it almost looked like an outline in a reverse silhouette.

After pulling in the garage, I stepped out of my car and went to the side of the garage and stood in the shadow so I couldn't be seen. There was a bright moon out and it was casting enough moonlight and I could clearly see. The creature's height was probably around seven feet tall. It was covered in shaggy hair, maybe four or five inches long. The hair looked thicker on its shoulders and over the top of its head. The head was large and oval-shaped. The face wasn't covered in hair, and I was able to see that its face was wide and flat. It also had a very flat nose. It didn't really seem to have lips; they were very thin. The bottom lip did seem to stick out a bit further than the upper lip, almost like it had an overbite.

The elevation drops off by the tree line. The creature's lower part of its body was hidden because of the elevation, the trash cans and a small storage shed at the back of the property. I could tell that it was "massive" in size, and it had incredibly long arms.

I just stood there, and I watched the creature raise its right arm before turning and walking away, morphing into the dense woods, and disappearing into the shadows near the creek. I knew that the woods were very thick and difficult to travel through during the day. The creature didn't seem to have any problem maneuvering through them at night and disappeared quickly into the darkness. I watched for the creature for about one minute. When it looked like he was gone and not returning, I stepped out of the shadow of the garage and closed the door, then quickly ran inside.

I was confident that what I had seen was not a human, but I thought that it might be a trespasser. Given the recent break-ins within the community and the theft of holiday gifts, I honestly thought this might be the robber, but then thinking about its physical characteristics, behavior, and sheer size left me convinced that it wasn't human.

I rushed inside to call the sheriff and tell him what had just happened. I called and he said he would come out and check things out. I stepped out of the back door of my house and turned on the exterior lights. While I was standing on the porch, I noticed a most peculiar odor. It was like a bad skunk had been frightened and sprayed something. That's the odor that was drifting through the air.

It wasn't long before the sheriff arrived. I met him in the driveway and told him what I had seen and pointed out where the creature had been. The sheriff told me to go back inside, so I went back and stood on the porch. I watched him take out the flashlight and search around the property. He also investigated the windows of the house to make sure no one had broken in. While walking around, he discovered three distinct footprints in the flower beds. They were near the boat shed in the back. These footprints measured a considerable 18 inches in length and were barefoot. The person or creature who made these prints wasn't wearing any shoes. The sheriff later told me that was the thing that stuck out to him - it was December and someone or something was walking around barefoot in the yard. He said the prints were rather fresh too. As I stood next to the sheriff back on my porch, I told him that the creature was approximately the same size as the tree in my yard, which would have made the creature to be around seven or eight feet tall.

THREE
OHIO SIGHTING

I KNOW there are a lot of people out there who believe that the Grassman, specifically the one in Ohio, is nothing more than a different breed of bigfoot but I honestly don't think so and I have had encounters with both. I also know that there are more than one kind of bigfoot creatures out there, but I can only keep this encounter in line with my own experiences and don't want to speculate. I grew up in Ohio in a very rural area and it wasn't unusual for me to play in the woods or go fishing by a creek that ran all throughout the woods that surrounded my house. Even as I got older, I would be in the woods a lot and have encountered bigfoot on more than one occasion. Most of the time it was hardly an encounter, and it took place at night, but I know it was bigfoot and not the Grassman because the shape of them differs greatly and, bigfoot seemed benevolent to me. I know there's been a lot of reports about bigfoot with all different colored hair or fur but the ones I always saw had brownish-red fur and aside from making some very aggressive noises and oftentimes throwing rocks if we got too close to what they were claiming as their territory, they never attacked or approached us. I've seen them walking around in the woods and the moment they would see me and/or whoever else I happened to be with now they would run away and seemed like they wanted to get as far away from us as possible. It will sound strange to a lot of people but seeing and encountering bigfoot was a part of life and nothing that we ever got bent out of shape about and after the first few times we just started ignoring it as best as we could, and it gave us the same courtesy. However, what I am about to tell you about now is the Grassman and it's a creature we didn't know existed until very recently, or at least we didn't know there was a name for it. By "we" I am referring to me and my family, as we have all seen both creatures at one point or another.

It started when we moved into a much bigger house. My dad got a crazy promotion at work, and we were able to move into a huge house in a much more affluent area of Ohio. It was great, especially as a teenager, to be able to have so much space and room. We lived with my grandparents on and off and were in and out of rental homes my whole childhood. Once we moved into the new house, a whole new world opened for us, and we never expected that an unknown and deadly creature would be what we had to worry about when it seemed like everything else was finally falling into place. The new house was situated on several acres of land, and it was surrounded by very dense woods. There weren't any neighbors in the general vicinity and the house was on a large hill, kind of overlooking the valley and other homes below. You would have had to drive about forty minutes to get from the bottom of the hill where the town and the other houses were to get to our house, and we loved it. We had an in-ground pool in the backyard and plenty of places for me and my dad and brothers to go fishing whenever the mood struck us. It was isolated but after living in such proximity to so many loud and annoying neighbors our whole lives, or sharing a home with other people, it really felt like a whole new world for all of us. That is until our new home went from being a place where we felt safe and at peace to a place of terror and never knowing what was going to happen next.

My siblings and I all had our own rooms in the new house and mine was the only one on the first floor of the house. I took one of the back rooms that would normally serve as a den, but I liked it because it had two sliding glass doors that looked out over the side of the house and the woods and one of the walls was covered in windows. I put black out curtains up, and blinds, and I was in my own little heaven. It was about six months after we moved in that everything started to get weird. One more than one occasion I was woken up in the middle of the night to the sound of something banging very aggressively on the side of the house. I could hear it from where I was sleeping but it was the side of the house that my bedroom wasn't connected to and by the time I would get up and make my way over to the room connected to that side of the house and look out the window, the noises would stop. After about a week of that happening I woke up one night to someone banging on my window in my bedroom. I immediately jumped up and looked out the window and screamed at the top of my lungs as I saw a set of eyes staring back at me. I fell backwards off my bed and my mom and dad came running into my room, turning all the lights on in the house on their way from their bedroom upstairs to mine. I was absolutely panicked but when my dad pulled back the curtains again on that same exact window, there was nothing there. He went out and walked around the house with a gun but there was also no one and nothing out there either. I personally think all the lights in the house going on and all the commotion alerted it to the fact that someone had seen it and it took off running. Obviously, it knew I had seen it, but I hadn't turned any lights on, and it probably wasn't scared of one human being. The very next day we noticed our German shepherd was missing.

I looked all around the yard and in the woods surrounding the house and eventually found her. She had been killed and I will just leave it at that because it still makes me sad to think about it and her death had been gruesome on top of it. We buried the dog on our property and that night I heard strange grunting sounds in the woods, but I didn't bother to look and see what was going on. I had developed, and still have this fear today, an intense fear of looking out windows at nighttime. I know it sounds ridiculous but maybe you've never seen strange and animalistic, violent looking eyes staring back at you when you looked out one. If that's ever happened to you then you know what I'm talking about. The next day the dog had been dug up and we never found her body. I am trying to put as much information as I can into this one encounter story so bear with me as I leave out a few minor details. We all knew there was something seriously wrong with the house or at least with something that was in the woods connected to the property, but we all chose to explain and rationalize it away. We essentially chose to just ignore it. One night I was home alone, and I wanted to go for a swim. We didn't have that many lights out on the deck or by the pool, but the pool had lights in it, so it was illuminated enough that I felt like I didn't need a flashlight. I heard an incredibly loud splash and those same grunting noises as I just described to you, and I heard it all as I was walking outside and to the pool. I immediately saw a huge figure running, soaking wet from the pool into the woods. I ran over once it was gone and saw that it left wet footprints all around the pool. The footprints looked like they could've belonged to bigfoot but the creature I had seen running away had black fur. I was terrified, of course, but being a teenage boy, I tried not to let it get to me and certainly didn't show it. About a week later my two youngest siblings came running inside of the house screaming and crying, saying a large man had been standing and watching them from the woods. My father and I immediately went outside and that was the first time we laid eyes on what we were dealing with. It was only about five foot seven inches tall, but it had to have weighed at least three hundred pounds. It just stood there, next to a giant tree, right at the tree line where the property met the forest, and it just stared at us. We stared back at it, not knowing what else to do.

The creature pounded its chest in what seemed like a very aggressive manner and took off back into the woods. My grandparents were visiting and reported seeing the same creature staring at them from the wood while they were relaxing in the lounge chairs by the pool too. We had seen it, but we still didn't know what we were really dealing with. We were all certain that what-ever it was had killed our dog and now it was terrorizing the whole family. However, a few months went by without there being any sightings or abnormal activity and eventually things calmed down enough that I wanted to do some night fishing. That wasn't abnormal and so I got my things together and went off into the woods. I knew the moment I entered the woods that something was very wrong. It was too quiet and too dark. It was nighttime, yes, but it was darker than that. It seemed unnatural somehow, like there was a dark and malevolent presence that brought its own absence of light with it wherever it went. I knew it was the creature and I knew it was watching me. I did my best to make believe I hadn't noticed anything was amiss and planned wholeheartedly on shooting the thing the moment I saw it. I knew it had the capacity to kill and I also knew it was vicious and hated human beings, don't ask me how but I simply just knew that. This wasn't bigfoot that we were dealing with. It was something much more sinister and much darker. I kept on walking towards the water and as I did, I heard a very loud and terrifying cry pierce the air and echo through the woods around me. It sounded like a mix between a baby crying and a woman screaming for her life. I got the chills and looked around to see if I could spot the thing that made the noise. It blended right into the woods, but I saw a set of reddish-orange eyes looking out at me from some very tall grass in between some trees. It made the mistake of blinking and finally I spotted it. I grabbed my gun and put down all my gear, prepared for a standoff with the entity or whatever it was. I was scared, don't get me wrong, but I was angrier and more upset than anything else. That thing had been terrorizing us for so long, I was finally ready to just get rid of it altogether. I wasn't thinking of having proof of its existence and honestly hadn't thought much past killing it. However, almost as if it knew what I was thinking, or maybe it merely recognized that I was aiming a deadly weapon at it, it stood up.

It started pushing on one of the smaller trees near it and I swear to you the tree started bending. It was looking right at me while it did that. Then, after it nearly snapped the whole tree in half by simply pushing on it with its weight, it started banging on some of the other trees. The banging loudly echoed all around me, but it was suddenly coming from several different places and the horrible cries were also coming from all over the woods. It wasn't alone. I realized right then that there was a group or family of them and that they would kill me in a heartbeat if I didn't get the hell out of there right away. I turned and walked as quickly as I could out of those woods and the next day my father and some of his friends went out there with guns, but they never could find the creatures. The harassment went on for years and there wasn't anything we could ever do about it either. No one believed us except other people in town who had almost hit it when it jumped out in front of and then attacked their cars and the local authorities didn't help at all either. Then, one day it all just stopped, and we didn't have any activity for years. It starts and stops suddenly but we never got another pet and even now, I live very close to that big house on the hill where my parents still live, I won't have any pets and I don't allow my children to play outside. There's a ferocious and terrible monster that lurks out there, more than one of them, and I believe that they are responsible for the deaths of many animals and livestock in the area. However, upon doing further research, I believe that they are also energy vampires and feed off terror and lower vibrational human emotions. That's just my theory but it is based on a lot of experience. I left some stuff out of this encounter and tried to just list some of the times when we came across the so-called Grassman. It isn't bigfoot and is a whole other type of being. That's the only thing I know with absolute certainty.

FOUR
CALIFORNIA SIGHTING

I HAVE SPENT most of my life in the wilderness, for one thing or another, but mostly it was playing when I was a kid and camping and hiking now that I'm an adult. I have seen and heard some strange things throughout the years, but I'll never forget something that happened to me while I was on a family camping trip, and I had gone off on my own to go swimming. The encounter wasn't terrifying, on its own, but what I saw and heard terrified me, nonetheless. Thinking back on it I wish I would have investigated further and not been as scared as I was. However, I was only around nine years old and had never heard about bigfoot before. I think people knew about bigfoot, but it was just a legend to everyone I knew, and I was too young for anyone to have informed me about it anyway, even if they had been believers. My family and I lived in southern California in the United States, and we were visiting the northern part of the state and camping in the forest around the mountains. It was something we did all the time and I always enjoyed it. I also played in the woods around my house too. My life was typical of a young boy back in those days and I never expected anything out of the ordinary to happen to me at any given time. I was lucky, I guess, looking back on it now because it was only bigfoot I had come across. I know better now, with the invention and some exploration of the internet, that there are oftentimes much worse things out there in the wilderness.

We had been to this campsite before and while it wasn't ever really crowded, there were always other people there. I remember there were always other kids my age to play with and that was one of the things I enjoyed most about the whole vacation. It was the end of the summer and there was a spot to swim and all around there my family and other families who were out camping there would all barbeque and drink beer and wine and just have a great time. They would blast music and there were never any problems. On the third night of our trip, my father asked me and another kid, one I didn't know and who was at least five years older than me, to go and collect some kindling from the woods. I agreed right away but the other kid had to be forced to go and really seemed like he didn't want to. He reluctantly agreed and when I asked him why he feared the woods, he started telling me all about the demons and ghosts that haunted that area. Of course, he was just trying to scare me but there was bothering him about being in the woods at night with only someone like me, who I'm sure he considered to be a baby compared to him. He was nice to me though, despite the teasing and when he saw me stop in my tracks and my eyes go wide, he laughed and shuffled my hair and told me he had only been joking. So, being a kid, I asked him what really scared him about the woods, and he said he believed it was haunted for real, but that he hadn't ever seen anything. I was immediately terrified. I shined my flash-light and jumped at every single noise, even the normal ones in the forest that I was very used to. I just wanted to get the kindling and get out of there and the other kid agreed with me.

We heard strange sounds, almost like whistling, the whole time we were collecting the wood out there. At first, we thought it was coming from our parents and all the others who were partying at the lake, but it got to the point where we were too far away from them to be able to put the blame on them. He and I grabbed what we could and ran back to the water. My dad asked what was wrong and we told him about the whistling. I think the adults had a little too much to drink at that point because my dad not only told me I was being silly, but he also laughed. The kid and I tried to explain that it wasn't like a normal person whistling and seemed somehow strange and like it didn't belong. He tried to convince us it was an owl, but we knew better. The whistling had lasted a full thirty seconds or more before it stopped and another one came. It was what it was though and eventually I somewhat forgot about it. The music and the party were so loud, no one else would have heard it anyway. Eventually the night ended, and we all walked back to camp. I was scared the whole way and once we were in the middle of the forest and only halfway to our camp, the whistling started again. Everyone heard it and we all stopped but no one really seemed to think there was anything weird about it, so we just kept on moving and eventually went to sleep. The incessant whistling became a problem when it was so persistent and so loud, for hours in the middle of the night, that no one could sleep. My dad said he was going to ask one of the rangers or security what the heck was making that racket. Eventually, at around three in the morning, it stopped completely and for the rest of the night. Nothing about this would have been scary had that kid not told me about supposed demons and alleged lost souls wandering around. I knew he was kidding, kind of, but at that age I really thought that maybe it was a demon that was whistling. It sounded terrific and I thought how I would have loved to have been able to whistle like that.

The next morning, we woke up and had breakfast.

We got ready to go swimming, but my little sister wasn't feeling well suddenly. I was impatient and could only think about getting out of the blazing heat and into the water. My dad got annoyed with me and called me inconsiderate, but my mother told me to just go on ahead. It was morning and so while I was still a little spooked about the whistling the night before, I didn't think anything could or would happen to me out there alone while the sun was out. Apparently, my parents didn't either because up to that point I had never been allowed to go anywhere alone when we were camping or otherwise in the woods. I walked quickly, trying to get there fast so I could cool off. It was around ninety degrees and only like ten o'clock in the morning. It was going to be hot all day. As I walked, I got the distinct impression that I was not only being watched but followed as well. I looked all around but didn't see anything at first. It took about ten minutes of having the overwhelming feeling that I wasn't alone before finally I went off trail a little bit to see if maybe it was some sort of animal or something. As soon as I was off the trail, I heard the familiar, long whistling sounds from the night before. I stopped dead in my tracks and looked over towards where it sounded like it was coming from. There was a huge boulder over to my right, about three yards away from me, and something was sitting on it. At first, I thought it was a large man but then I shielded my eyes from the sun and saw that it wasn't. It was what had been whistling though. It just sat there, looking at me and whistling. I wanted to scream and run away but something deep inside of me, probably my intuition or instinct, told me not to do that. I knew as well that running from any sort of large or predatory animal would almost certainly make them give chase and this thing was so foreign and so tremendously big that I knew I didn't stand a chance. All I could do was stare at it as it stared at me. I didn't even want to break eye contact.

It was covered in black fur, but it had some white patches to it, all over its body. It sat there, just like a normal human being would, with its legs over the side of the boulder. It kept whistling and staring at me and it started to get very creepy, but I didn't know what to do. The strangest thing about it all, and I still think about this to this very day, was the odd grin it had on its face when it would take a break for a moment from whistling. It looked somewhat like a gorilla or an ape, but it also looked like a man. It had very long hair on and around its head, but the face had no hair at all. I couldn't see the color of its eyes but there was something in them that looked human, and it was also in the way that he was sitting, whistling, and grinning at me. It was almost like he was getting a kick out of freaking me out. I relaxed a little and started to back away. That was a bad idea, or so it seemed, because the creature got off the boulder and stood up and that's when I finally saw just how huge it was. It stood at least thirteen feet tall, maybe taller. Its arms hung down below its knees and instead of grinning, it looked angry. It wasn't whistling anymore but glaring at me, as though I had somehow insulted it by not continuing to stand there and listen to it. It growled once and then climbed up a nearby tree. I kept my eyes shielded as I watched it and just like an ape or like something you would have seen in a movie about Tarzan or something, it jumped from tree to tree, somehow still whistling all the way. I breathed a heavy sigh of relief and turned to run. I ran all the way back to my camp to tell my dad what had just happened to me.

I couldn't blame it on the alcohol the next day as he was sober and still wasn't understanding me or maybe he just didn't want to hear what I was saying. He was convinced it was nothing more than a man and that my imagination had gotten the better of me. I was angry and pleaded with him to believe me, but he didn't. In fact, it took almost thirty years and a lot of me bringing him research into bigfoot and other woodland creatures that are said to be somewhat supernatural in nature, before he finally relented and told me he had believed me all along. What I had suspected was right. Seeing the bigfoot, which I didn't know what it was at the time, changed me and I have been fascinated with them and others ever since. I wouldn't say I go out of my way to hunt or find them or anything like that, but I do always hope to see one when I am in the woods. I wish I would have taken two steps forward instead of two steps back, but I also know better. I've learned they're normally very territorial and aggressive if you get too close and I wonder if my being a small, little kid had anything to do with how calm it was with me. Well, it was calm for the most part. I will never forget that sneaky grin that was on its face though. The one that told me it was enjoying messing with me and just having a good time. I didn't see anything else for the rest of that trip and neither did anyone else in my family. We didn't hear any more whistling either but when my dad approached the rangers when we were on our way out and asked them about what the whistling noise was and where it was coming from, they shrugged and said they hadn't ever heard it. I wonder if they were grinning as we drove away, knowing full well what it had been that was making the noises, and that the joke was on us. I didn't tell the rangers what I had seen.

`

FIVE
TEXAS SIGHTING

IT WAS EARLY in the summer of 1987 when I had my encounter with Bigfoot. I was living on my family's farm in a little town called Shelbyville that was in deep East Texas. In that part of the country, we have family cemeteries and we each took care of our own family's graves, weeding and mowing and taking care of the area. It was hot that summer so I had to wait until it would cool off, so later in the evening before dark, I would get on my tractor and head up to the cemetery. To stay off the road, I would drive down the gravel on the side or in the ditch. I lived here my entire life, so this was expected of me, and I did it without hesitation. My family had several acres that we still lived on. I had several deer feeders on our property, so I was familiar with the type of animals we had living near us and the sounds that they made.

I was driving down the side of the road and getting

close to the turnoff that led to the cemetery. It was a dirt road that led up to the gate and I would have to stop and open the gate, pull through and then close it again. Before I got to the gate, I spotted something moving across the pasture in front of me. The road was about 15 feet wide there and went from tree line to tree line. I had my 3-year-old hound dog with me in the trailer attached to the tractor. She started to act differently and not like herself at all. She started to bark like crazy and then it suddenly turned into a fearful whimper.

I slowed down the tractor and I saw something right before me. Crossing the road was a huge, hairy figure that looked like Bigfoot! This creature walked across the road and went over to the next pasture. It only had to take a couple of steps before it made it over to the cover of the tree line. It had a huge stride and it walked across 40 yards in just a few steps. Though I had seen depictions of Bigfoot on television I really didn't think they were real or at least, they didn't live around here. I'd been here my entire life and I never saw anything like that before.

The creature that crossed the road was a tall, hairy being, walking upright like a man. It was walking on two legs, just swinging its arms as it went on its way. It walked quite swiftly. As it walked it looked like a human. I was getting uneasy and so was my dog as we both watched this creature. I was overwhelmed. I didn't smell any strange odors, but I think my dog might have. She had her nose up in the air and was sniffing like crazy. I couldn't be certain though. By the time I got up to where I saw the creature on the road, the wind had shifted and was blowing out of the southeast, putting me upwind of the creature.

When I got to the spot where I saw the creature crossed the trail, I stopped my tractor and cut off the engine. I wanted to see if there were any more traces of the creature lingering around. I listened for any yells or screams or branches snapping and breaking. The only sound I heard was the whine of my dog in the trailer. It was strange, but the woods were unusually quiet. There were no bird sounds or any other animals for that matter. I had a very uneasy feeling, and I restarted the tractor. I decided to leave and come back another time to finish up in the cemetery.

Riding back home, I started to remember my mother's stories from her childhood. She often said that she saw Bigfoot when she was a little girl. She told me about one time when a large and shadowy form had been walking behind a trellis in her backyard one afternoon. She used to tell me that the creature stood very tall and might have been eight or nine feet tall. She said that its head and shoulders were visible above the trellis itself.

To my knowledge, none of my neighbors had shared similar experiences or reported related sightings of

Bigfoot on their properties. I do remember the time my father and I heard what sounded like a panther screaming in the woods. At least he told me it was a panther. It sounded like a woman screaming out because she was being attacked. We looked around that night but never found anyone who needed help or being attacked. While I had never encountered a panther firsthand, I have seen their tracks in the Piney Woods, so I know they are in the area.

SIX
COLORADO SIGHTING

IN LATE OCTOBER OF 1992, I was living and going to school in Colorado. It was the first time I was really on my own and I found I was making friends quickly and easily. There was one day that was particularly beautiful and two of my friends mentioned they wanted to go hiking in Grand Mesa. I had always wanted to visit that area and they quickly invited me along for the afternoon. The three of us set off on a hiking adventure, unaware of what we would eventually run into.

I packed up and was ready. We hit the trail and went about a mile or so. Then we suddenly heard a growl! I didn't know where it was coming from. It echoed in the wilderness. At first, I thought it was a black bear. When I said that it might be a bear, we all reached for our bear spray and looked around us, trying to find where the growl was coming from.

From deep in the trees, I could hear rustling and branches breaking. I knew something was coming our way. Within a few seconds, a huge figure emerged from the woods and stepped on the trail in front of us. It was at least seven feet tall and was covered in long. It was standing firmly on two legs and wasn't wearing clothes or any type of collar or leash. It was a wild animal. It was about 25 or 30 yards in front of us. Its eyes locked onto mine and I was terrified and couldn't move. My friends were frozen too.

The creature just stood there and looked at us. It opened its mouth and made the most intense yell I've ever heard. The scream echoed through the air. If I hadn't been so terrified, I would have been impressed at the power of the yell. After it yelled, it looked at us again, then it pivoted and took one more step across the trail. It disappeared back into the wilderness, but on the other side of the trail. We all stood in stunned silence, trying to make sense of what we had just seen.

The creature stood on two legs like it was a human. It was tall, taller than any animal I had ever seen. It was at least seven feet tall, maybe eight. It had a distinctive cone-shaped head that was covered in a thick jagged hair, and it had long red-auburn hair that went down its back. Its eyes were very narrow and dark black. The face had an overall flat shape to it, except for the ridge above the eyes. That was almost ape-like. I didn't see any ears on the creature, but that could be because the head was covered with hair. The nose was wide and flat, and its lips were rather thin. The bottom lip stuck out a bit more, and when it yelled, I could see a mouth full of sharp and jagged teeth. I realized I was only able to see its upper teeth because it tilted its head back when it screamed. It had long arms and really no neck to describe. When it walked across the trail it was able to cross in two steps. The arms just hung and swung by its sides as it walked by. The creature had a most disturbing smell too, something like a rancid sewer and dead animals mixed.

I just looked at the sheer size of the creature. It scared the breath out of us. We were all filled with terror. We ran the entire distance back to our cars. Once we got back, we swore we'd never hike in this area again.

We had agreed to not tell any of our school friends, but I knew I needed to tell someone, just so I could get it off my chest. I didn't want to tell my new Colorado friends. I knew they would think I was slightly off my rocker. Eventually, I confided in my father. I told him about all the events that had happened and all the details I could remember. I thought my dad, who had experiences of his own when he was a child, would be more open minded and let his friends know that there was something on their property. The area of the trail that my friends and I were hiking on was on my father's friend's property, which was off-limits to the public. When I told him, he responded with skepticism, which made me think that maybe his experiences were not real after all, and he made them up.

Since it was on private property, I was unable to return to the scene of the incident. I'm not sure if my father relayed the information to his friends or not. In any case, I never went back or had any more Bigfoot sightings while I lived in Colorado.

SEVEN
WEST VIRGINIA SIGHTING

IN THE SUMMER OF 1983, my boyfriend was a long-haul truck driver. We moved back to the farm in Bemis, West Virginia to help his mom, who was a widow now. Many nights I was home alone when Brad was out driving. Mom lived in the farmhouse and Brad, and I had a trailer about 60 yards behind her house.

This was just like any other night. It was getting close to 8 PM and Mom was in in her house, probably getting ready for bed. I was in our trailer watching TV. I was sitting on the sofa, and I started to smell a putrid odor. The window nearest to me in the living room was open, so I closed it the entire way. I looked around, trying to find where the smell was coming from, but the smell vanished as quickly as it had appeared.

A few minutes later, the stench returned and was even stronger than before. I couldn't take it this time, so I got up and closed the rest of the windows in the trailer. About that time, my little sister, who was visiting for the weekend, walked in and smelled it too. We were walking around the living room, trying to find the smell. She noticed the window in the kitchen was open a bit. She saw the breeze make the curtain move. Since the other window was open, I thought that the source of the stench must be from the outside. We closed all the windows downstairs hoping that would stop the odor. I went and got a can of air freshener and sprayed it around and everything was fine.

About an hour later, I went outside to feed the dogs. While I was out there, I saw someone standing not too far from mom's house, near the barbed wire fence. The person was standing in the dark, just watching her home. I stopped to look to see if it was someone I knew, but I didn't recognize the person. The person was unusually large which frightened me since mom was probably in bed already. I came back in and turned on all the lights outside, including the large one over the barn. I immediately told my sister to get dressed and I went and called the sheriff.

Within a couple of minutes, two sheriff deputies arrived at our property with their lights flashing. They walked around, shining their mag light flashlights everywhere and lit up the yard. Despite their search, no trace of the person was found. They left but said they would check back in the morning to make sure everything was still ok.

I was worried about mom, who was alone inside. I saw her bedroom light was still on, so I knew she was awake. I called her on the phone and told her what happened. She too went and turned all her exterior lights on and closed her windows and doors. She said she hadn't seen anyone, but she'd sleep with the house and yard lit up. I told her that my sister and I would come over and stay with her if she wanted. We all agreed that would be the best thing.

I felt that everything was ok, and I was getting ready to go to sleep. My sister went into Brad's old room to sleep, and I decided to take the sofa in the living room. I went into the kitchen for a glass of water and a snack. When I looked out the window over the sink, I saw a big, dirty, hairy man without any clothes on walking around. He was close to seven feet tall and had long arms that went past his knees. I thought maybe someone was pranking us at first. I dismissed that thought and I didn't waste a second and called the sheriff's office again. In under three minutes, I heard sirens and saw the flashing lights soon thereafter. They weren't playing around this time.

The deputies were back and jumped out of their car, flashlights in their hands. They looked everywhere. They found no trace of the intruder. Knowing that there were three females alone on the farm, they assured us that they would patrol the area throughout the night. Then they left. I knew they kept patrolling around through the night. There were several times I saw their lights flash through the window in the living room.

After the sheriff left the second time, I called a friend of my boyfriend's, Tony. My boyfriend and Tony had been friends since childhood and a lot of times they would go fishing or hunting together. Tony always kept an eye out for us when Brad was out on the road. Brad and Tony had lived here their entire lives and I knew if anyone had ever seen or heard about something like this, it would be Tony. Tony answered the phone, and I started to tell him about the big hairy man walking around the yard. Tony listened and let me get it all off my chest and then he said he didn't want to scare me. He said, especially since my sister and I had smelled the horrible stench earlier, it most likely was Bigfoot. Tony told me that Bigfoot stays out in the yard and doesn't attack people, or at least he's never heard of a story about Bigfoot attacking anyone. If we stayed inside and kept the outside lights on, we would be fine. That is what I did, and I never saw the hairy man again.

EIGHT
PENNSYLVANIA SIGHTING

LIVING in the Bethlehem region of the Lehigh Valley in Northeast PA, the idea of Sasquatch sightings was almost a foreign concept to me. You see, this part of Pennsylvania is teeming with people, and Philadelphia isn't far off. So the idea of spotting such a creature here seemed highly improbable. However, my experience challenges that belief.

My friend and I, being enthusiastic campers and backpackers, had ventured into many parts of Pennsylvania and its neighboring areas. An interesting feature here is the Appalachian Trail, which runs very close to where we live. The Bake Oven Knob, a renowned lookout spot on the trail, offered a panoramic view of the valley. From here, our favorite route led north/northeast along the Appalachian Trail, continuing till we reached Route 209. Our journey would then divert north/northwest into the Delaware Water Gap, briefly crossing into New Jersey before heading north into the gap. Our end goal was the Promised Land State Park, although we didn't always make it due to navigational challenges. This was an era where smartphones with GPS weren't the norm, so we relied heavily on maps, compasses, and recognizable landmarks. After leaving the defined trails of the Appalachian, our journey became more of trail-blazing through dense underbrush.

During one of these adventures, just as the sun was preparing to dip below the horizon, we halted to set up camp. The dense foliage made it challenging to find a suitable spot. We happened to be on a game trail, which seemed well-trodden. As we paused, a swampy odor engulfed the air, a mix of rotting vegetation and stagnant water. Curious, I slashed through some bushes on the trail's left with my machete, hoping to find the source of the smell. Unexpectedly, a creature – mere feet away from us – dashed away, making a thunderous noise reminiscent of a large vehicle crashing through the woods. The sound was distinctive; not like any deer or bear we'd ever encountered. This creature moved with an unbelievable speed and seemed to plow down thickets and even small trees in its haste.

I mustered the courage to inspect the area and was taken aback when I caught a fleeting glimpse of what seemed like a large, dark humanoid figure leaping into a ravine. The creature's outstretched arms spanned roughly eight feet, and while I couldn't decipher any intricate details due to the speed of its retreat, I was certain its silhouette was more human than animal. But its size and strength were unlike any human I'd ever heard of.

The incident unnerved us deeply. We hastily found a clearing to camp for the night, though our chosen spot was far from ideal. Signs of animals bedding down were evident in the matted grass around us. That night was restless; we constantly heard rustling, branches snapping, and unidentifiable noises close by. Each time, we'd shout warnings, hoping to deter any wild animals. Yet, a mysterious incident further heightened our fear. A heavy log, untouched by fire, was found at the center of our campfire come morning – as if deliberately placed there by some unseen entity.

We've since returned to that area numerous times, but nothing out of the ordinary has occurred. Still, I often ponder about that night. It's feasible that a creature could traverse from places like Ohio, moving through the Allegheny National Forest, into the Delaware Water Gap, and further onto the Appalachian Trail. While this remains speculative, that experience certainly made me question the known – and the unknown – of our world.

NINE
UNDISCLOSED LOCATION

WHEN I WAS A LITTLE BOY, I spent a lot of time in the woods because I lived in a home that was surrounded by a forest. The forest around my house was beautiful and I remember feeling like a prince in a fairy-tale every time I stepped foot in it. Having grown up in this area themselves, my parents also loved to do things with us kids and by themselves, in the wilderness outside of our house. Even when we weren't in the woods, we were always outside doing something or another and every year when we would go on vacation in the summer, we would inevitably find ourselves somewhere like in the mountains or some other forested area, somewhere else, away from our home. We just loved to be outside in general and we engaged in many different activities out there as a family. One of the things my dad and I specifically liked to do was go canoeing and that's what we were doing the day we had our encounter with what we both believe to have been sasquatch or, bigfoot, depending on where you come from. I believe the two are one and the same and therefore might use them interchangeably throughout this story. My dad and I invited my sister and mom to go with us but neither one of them wanted to go that day, so we got into our truck and headed about an hour's drive away to a national park area where we were able to rent a canoe and take it out for the day. I was excited because we had only ever been canoeing twice before and it was fun both of those times. Plus, it wasn't often my dad and I got to do things where it was just me and him so that made it even more special. We didn't go into the forest that day expecting to see bigfoot but we both knew the legends of bigfoot very well. Growing up in a rural and heavily wooded town like we did, there wasn't much you could do to avoid hearing about it. My dad believed that people were seeing something, he just wasn't sure if he could wrap his head around it being a giant ape-like creature that was bipedal and whose face was said to resemble that of a caveman and I didn't care one way or another if it was true or not and just hoped and prayed that if it was true I never had to see one first hand. All in all, though, I'm glad I did see one, but I wasn't at the time.

The lake we were canoeing on was well stocked with

plenty of fish and my dad and I bought some bait and decided to throw our lines in and see what we could catch while we were out there. We planned on making a whole day of it and had gotten there early. We were just casting out our lines at eleven in the morning. Even though dad taught me about the catch and release method of fishing, it was still exciting to make it a little competition between us to see who could catch the most fish and the largest fish of the day. We were having a good time and we were whispering, so as not to scare the fish. The water was very calm and there wasn't much of a breeze. It wasn't too hot and all in all it was shaping up to be the perfect day for a father and son to spend some time out in the wilds of nature together. We were catching fish left and right and we had little buckets to keep them in until we counted them and released them back into the water. We weren't paying much attention to our surroundings or much else other than one another and we were shocked when something made a huge splash in the water, almost landing in the canoe and that almost caused enough waves that we nearly tipped. We both jumped and looked around but didn't see anything at first. It had startled us, and my dad was immediately on high alert. Seeing him like that made me more fearful and I just sat there still and quiet while we looked around to see what had just almost hit us. We were far enough into the water that nothing could have fallen from anywhere and someone had to have thrown some-thing. Even the trees were too far away for anything to have fallen from them. Not to mention, whatever it was, it had been huge and there was nothing we could think of that would have been falling from those trees that would have been that big. Suddenly my dad told me to duck, and I did so, immediately, and he did too. I managed to get a look at a gigantic rock that was headed our way and I was scared that we would be capsized should it have hit us. I followed my dad's gaze, once it too landed in the water and splashed around us, to where it had come from. I was shocked and terrified all at once by what we both saw.

We were looking at what at first appeared to be a giant, hairy, wild man swiftly and adeptly running down the slope to the water from the top of one of the surrounding cliffs. It was making all sorts of strange noises and halfway through its run it stopped and stared at us intently. It was obviously angry, whatever it was, and we both just sat there slack jawed, staring back at it. Once it was still it registered to my father first what we were looking at. He said a few curse words and I heard the word "sasquatch" in there somewhere. I took a deep breath and screamed. My dad gave me an angry look as the creature started pounding on its chest and bent down to pick up another giant-sized rock. It looked like a pebble in the thing's hand. It stood at around thirteen feet tall and was half as wide as that. It had giant hands and feet, was covered in brownish-red hair everywhere except the face and a little bit of the stomach and around the chest area, and it was very muscular. It looked like something that could have ripped us apart with its bare hands if it wanted to and it seemed a bit like that's exactly what it wanted to do. It didn't throw the third rock immediately and its long arms just hung there, past its knees and almost to its ankles. It was broad daylight outside and there was nothing obstructing our view of this thing. We were still having a hard time believing it nonetheless though, as I'm sure you can imagine. Its eyes looked black as it stared at us with a look of disgust on its face and making all sorts of inhuman and bizarre noises. Then, it started banging its other hand, the one not holding the rock, on one of the trees near it. Suddenly we heard thunderous sounds exactly like the ones that thing was making but coming from all different places around the forest surrounding where we sat, helplessly, in the water. Rocks of all shapes and sizes came flying into the water all around us, effectively almost tipping the boat. I say that because I believe they were trying to scare us and if they had wanted to hurt, kill, or capsize us they could have easily done so. My dad suddenly looked like he had an important idea or like something obvious had just dawned on him. "The fish," he said.

He grabbed the buckets and released the fish back into the water and the sasquatch, the one we could see, stopped running with the agility of a mountain goat, down the side of the mountain towards us. It roared and pounded its chest again and suddenly all the others were quiet, and our boat wasn't being almost tipped by all the huge rocks previously being tossed in the water anymore. Everything went eerily quiet. Suddenly some very large, boulder sized rocks came tumbling out of the side of the cliff and rolling towards the sasquatch. It dove into the water about two yards upstream from us and my dad took that as our cue to get the hell out of there. He and I started paddling the canoe as fast as we possibly could until we could no longer see the bigfoot, which by the way had been swimming right towards us when we rounded a little bend and couldn't see it anymore. It swam super-fast, too, just like it had been able to run along the rocky side of a cliff. It was graceful and agile, especially for how big it was. My dad and I couldn't get back to our car fast enough. When we brought the canoe back to the rental place, we told the guy there all about what we had just seen but he shrugged and laughed at us as though it was the silliest thing he had ever heard. However, it was obvious that he knew exactly what we were talking about because his eyes went wide before, he quickly tried to cover up his surprise and fear with his chuckling. He was scared but he wasn't surprised by what we told him we saw.

My dad and I couldn't relax until we were in the car and on our way back home. Then, we talked excitedly to one another about the experience and still couldn't believe it. He said it was the first time he had ever seen a sasquatch and that, despite how cool it was going to be to be able to tell the story to all his friends, he hoped to God it would be the last time he ever saw one. I agreed with him and both of us got our wish. This encounter didn't deter either one of us from doing what we had always done in the woods, and we still enjoyed our time together out there, both alone and with one another and others, but we were a lot more mindful of our surroundings from that day forward. My mother and sister first thought that we were trying to scare them but eventually believed us and I don't think either one of them ever went into the woods without either me or my dad again. He and I have spoken about that encounter more times than I could possibly count but we both tend to agree on several things. One, that it was indeed a sasquatch or bigfoot that we had encountered that day. The second thing is that it was territorial because we were more than likely canoeing somewhere near where it and the others lived. Third, it looked like we were taking a bunch of fish out of the freshly stocked water and it more than likely considered it to be their food, because that was their home. They thought we were stealing from them and taking food out of their mouths. I've never passed up the chance to tell this remarkable story and feel blessed that I got to see something like that, at least once in my lifetime. I have been seeing a lot of similar encounters online lately and thought there would be some people out there who might be interested in what I have to say and what I saw and experienced decades ago with regards to bigfoot. The more I read about them the more I realize our encounter was typical of sasquatch encounters. They have a thing for banging on trees and throwing rocks and I've come across more stories than I can even count where people have experienced those same two things during their encounters. It just goes to show that, just like human beings, they're creatures of habit too and if you don't respect their homes and their land, or if they feel you're trying to steal from them, just like with most humans, you will live to regret it.

TEN
KENTUCKY SIGHTING

IN 2022, I had one of the most surreal experiences of my life while deer hunting on our family property in eastern Kentucky with my eldest daughter. As a native of the Montgomery/Menifee line, hunting in the densely wooded expanse has been a tradition. My reticence to share this eerie tale stems from my inherent skepticism, but perhaps it's time to recount this otherworldly encounter.

Having promised my six-year-old daughter an adventure during the opening day of the modern gun season, we set out. The property that my husband, father and I own spans roughly 40 acres, cloaked almost entirely in trees. Our land stretches to the summit of Turkey Knob, beyond which lies a vast swath of untouched forest spanning hundreds of acres.

That particular morning, dawn was breaking as we

ventured into the woods. We were slightly delayed because I had been attending to our four-month-old baby and ensuring that my husband and young son had their breakfast. Given the growing daylight, I opted to situate ourselves at ground level rather than making the trek to our usual stand. We settled by a tree, perfectly positioned against the crest of Turkey Knob. From there, we had a clear view across the ravine to the ridge line marked by a prominent game trail.

After about 30 minutes, with my daughter dozing peacefully in my lap, my attention was drawn to a group of gray squirrels frolicking on a log downhill. The serene scene was disrupted by a sudden, faint cry reminiscent of a baby. At first, I dismissed it, attributing the phantom sound to my recent motherly duties, but then it echoed again. The once lively forest fell eerily silent, amplifying my confusion about the source of the cry.

As I strained to locate the cry, a thunderous sound, akin to the galloping of our horses, erupted from the mountain slope behind us. With my daughter still in slumber, I dared not move abruptly. Reaching cautiously for the knife by my side, I took a quick glance sideways, expecting to see a startled bear. However, what I witnessed defied all reason.

Emerging from behind a tree, a large creature with a thick black fur coat moved swiftly. As it came into full view, I realized this was no ordinary woodland creature.

Its face, while somewhat reminiscent of a bear, possessed distinctly human-like features. Our eyes locked in a moment of mutual surprise. The creature momentarily appeared to prepare for an aggressive move, but upon seemingly recognizing the vulnerability of my position, its demeanor shifted dramatically. It gently raised its large hands, as if to communicate peace, then slowly retreated, disappearing into the forest's dense foliage.

This towering figure, standing at around six feet with patches of gray skin on its face and hands, bore soulful human eyes. Its entire presence rendered me in a daze. Given the creature's unexpected gentleness, I felt an inexplicable bond, as if we were two mothers understanding the sacred vow to protect.

Although I remain unsure of the creature's identity, its female essence felt unmistakable. The bizarre nature of this event, coupled with other peculiar occurrences on our property, has left me hesitant to share, fearing the incredulity of others. But deep in the heart of eastern Kentucky's woods, I encountered an enigma that challenges our understanding of the natural world.

PUBLISHER'S EXCERPT

INTO THE DARKNESS

FACELESS CREATURE

I grew up in Arkansas and I lived basically in the middle of the woods. I don't mean to sound cliche because I read a lot of these encounter stories because I am always searching for answers to what I saw and I know that most of them start like that. It's true though and I think that has a lot to do with why I saw what I did. I feel like the forests and woods of the world are places where there are lines between realms and dimensions and sometimes things cross from one to another, whether on purpose or accidentally. Most of the time I don't think anyone notices but I believe that when human beings end up coming across something like what I saw, something unexplainable, that's one of the reasons why. We simply see something we shouldn't have and are then left to live the rest of our lives with that information and most of the time we have no idea what to even do with it all. I was seven years old and was camping in some woods by my house with my mom, dad and older sister. We went camping several times a year, usually with the change of the seasons and it never got boring or old for us. It was the nineteen sixties and there wasn't a lot to do otherwise. Not if you didn't have a lot of money anyway and my family definitely fit under that category. Now, I want to say right here and now that, as strange as it may sound, this was only the first of four times I saw something similar to what I'm about to describe to you. It came in a different guise every time and while this encounter was with "a little girl" it wasn't always that way. It did always happen in the same place though, this one patch of dense woods about a mile away from my grandparent's house. They lived a twenty minute drive from me and my parents and we visited with them a lot. I don't pretend to know what it all means but I wonder if I was chosen or, like I just said, if I just happened to be in the wrong place at the wrong time.

We left my grandparents house in the middle of the day. We had our campervan all packed up and ready to go. We didn't camp in tents anymore because my mom said my sister and I always had a really hard time when we would have to do it that way. I guess we didn't like lying in the dirt or whatever but she never really elaborated and simply said it made her job easier. We were familiar with the woods and spent a lot of time in the ones surrounding our house too. It was scary at night, I remember always feeling like something or someone was watching us. It was the first year we were using the campervan and my sister and I were very excited. We thought it was really fancy and didn't even want to leave it once we parked it in our campsite. My dad was an avid outdoorsman and wanted my sister and I to learn how to survive out there but I think he was giving in to my mom with the rental van. The first night there passed fairly normal and we were all in bed by eleven that night. The next day my mom asked my sister and I if we wanted to go and pick some berries with her. I eagerly said that I did but my sister had already agreed to go fishing with my dad. My mom grabbed some larger bushel baskets and we headed out on our way. We all agreed to meet back at the van in four hours in order to have lunch. Mom gave me my basket and told me not to stray too far away from her. I always wandered off as a kid. I liked to explore and while my parents encouraged that, my mother liked to always have her eyes on me. We picked berries for about an hour and suddenly I was really tired. My mom told me to sit on a large rock and stay with the bushels we had already almost filled while she went and just finished collecting enough berries to fill her last basket. I agreed to stay there and off she went.

My mom still swears she had only been gone ten minutes but in my memory she had been gone for so long I started to get really worried. I yelled out for her but she didn't answer me and so I screamed out to her but still received no answer. I had just started crying when I heard a noise coming from behind me. I heard giggling and turned around just in time to see a little girl in a white dress running away from me. I could only see her back but she had been wearing an old fashioned dress, even for the time it was then, and she had long, dark brown pigtails in her hair. They were braided. I ran after her and she continued to giggle and run deeper into the woods. The fact that I had told my mother I wouldn't move didn't even cross my mind. I was only seven years old and thought that I had found a new playmate. It didn't occur to my young brain that there shouldn't have been another unsupervised child out there, especially not one who was wearing a dress and who had such seemingly perfect hair. I yelled out to the little girl but she didn't turn around and after I chased her for almost five whole minutes, she turned a bend and seemed to have disappeared. I was confused but even worse than that I realized I had gotten lost while chasing her. I stood still and looked all around me but the woods looked a little different. How they looked different I couldn't quite put my finger on but the colors almost seemed brighter while the previously bright and sunny sky had gotten very dark. There were gray clouds in the sky and this only elevated my fear and confusion. I called out for my mother but again received no answer so I yelled for the little girl to come out. I had become convinced she was hiding from me. Just as I turned and started to walk the other way, I heard her giggling again. It was coming from behind one of the trees nearby. I ran over there and saw the same girl, on her knees and facing the tree. Her hands looked like they were in a praying position. I tapped her on the shoulder but she didn't even seem to know I was there. She didn't acknowledge me.

I was very annoyed and mad at the time because she had gotten me lost and then she was ignoring me. I grabbed her shoulder to try and get her to turn around and face me but it was the worst mistake of my life. She did turn around then but when she did I saw that she had no face. It wasn't like there were holes where her eyes and nose should've been but it just looked like nothing. Someone else who has encountered this same type of terrifying entity described it as looking like someone stretched a piece of fabric over a football. It was terrifying and I stumbled backwards and screamed. I was on my behind then and the little girl suddenly stood up. She was about five feet tall, so taller than I was, and she had white skin. Her arms were extremely long and her hands, while otherwise looking normal, hung down to her ankles. She took two steps towards me and stopped again as I tried to scoot back on my behind to get away from her. I didn't have enough room to stand up yet and also, my legs were far too shaky to even try to get up and get away. Then, as I screamed, the little girl turned her head to one side as though she were just staring at me and was very confused. All of this would have been enough but it got worse. She then started to mumble, as though she were trying to talk but her mouth was covered. It wasn't that it was covered so much that it wasn't there and I didn't know what to do. Finally, I couldn't take anymore and I got up to run. I heard the girl mumbling louder and incessantly as she followed behind me. She never ran but she walked very fast. It started to rain and I started to cry. I turned around to see if she was still chasing me and she was. I turned back around to watch where I was going so I didn't fall again and I slammed right into my father. He and my sister were making their way back from fishing. I screamed and fought with my dad to let me go before I realized who he was. He grabbed me and asked me what in the world I was doing. I snapped out of it.

I immediately looked behind me again but there was no one there. She had just been there a second ago and I realized too that it wasn't raining anymore. Not only that, I wasn't wet at all and it was almost as though it had never rained in the first place. I frantically tried to tell my dad and sister what had just happened to me. My sister thought I was just trying to scare her but my father looked more concerned than anything else. He asked me where my mother was and I told him I didn't know. We went back to the camp but my mom wasn't there either and we were in the middle of trying to figure out where we should go to try and find her when she came running through the woods. The minute she saw all of us she looked instantly relieved and ran over to me. She had tears in her eyes and it was like she couldn't believe what she was seeing. I tried once again to tell everyone what happened but none of them believed me. It turned out I had traveled nearly two miles from where we were berry picking to the area where my sister and father had been fishing. I had done that in a matter of mere minutes. Four and a half hours had passed which means I lost about two hours of time that I still have no memory of to this very day. My mom said she never went and didn't hear me far enough that she wouldn't have been able to hear me calling her at all. I got in a lot of trouble and wasn't allowed to participate in any of the fun activities with my dad and sister the whole next day. I had to stay in the campervan with my mom because they thought I had simply not listened to them and wandered off. However, none of them could explain how I had gotten so far in such a short amount of time, but I really don't think that they wanted to. It was all too much for them to handle.

I often wonder if I was abducted or something that day. The other three times I saw a similar faceless entity I also lost time, have no memory of what happened during the missing time and I had always seemed to travel much further than I should have been able to when looking for whatever image the entity presented itself as. I say that because I certainly don't believe I was dealing with an actual little girl, for obvious reasons. I think whatever lurked underneath the guise was pure evil and acted as some sort of lure. Whatever the reason and whomever the entities are, it all felt extremely nefarious to me from the moment I realized I was lost that first time. I don't talk about this in my private life or publicly and aside from trying to tell my parents and my sister that one time on the first day that it all happened, no one knows what happened to me. The other encounters happened throughout different times in my life. The second time I was a teenager and the other two times I was an adult already. It makes no rational sense, I know that, but there isn't anything to explain any of it otherwise either. It was terrifying and the implications of the distances traveled in such a short time in woodland areas I am usually very familiar with in general and the missing time are absolutely horrifying. I don't know if I was chosen or if I randomly stumbled upon the phenomenon and the powers that be, the ones who make these encounters possible and maybe even the ones behind the faceless entities, decided I was a good candidate for further experiences with them. It's all very confusing, I know, but that's really all there is to this particular encounter.

———

INTO THE DARKNESS, VOLUME 1

ELEVEN
ALASKA SIGHTING

I WAS BORN and raised in Alaska, and it's a place brimming with tales of the unknown. I currently live here with my wife and our four children. Alaska has always been a land of mysteries, legends, and wild tales, and one of the most persistent stories in our family revolves around Bigfoot.

My father, a respected Alaskan native artist, often combined travel with work. As a child, long drives through the expansive wilderness were common. He used these drives as opportunities to share stories and tales with me and my siblings. Among those tales, the legend of Bigfoot stood out. He firmly believed in its existence, describing distant encounters or the tales he'd heard from fellow locals.

One of the most vivid memories from my childhood is from a trip we took when I was around 12. We were on our way from Anchorage to Fairbanks, a journey that cuts through some of the most pristine and untouched parts of Alaska. We decided to camp beside a serene river, its clear waters reflecting the night sky. As we sat by the campfire, a sudden, loud splash disrupted the peaceful night. It sounded distinctly like a large rock had been thrown into the water. We all turned our heads instantly towards the river, our faces lit with a mix of curiosity and concern. My dad, with a half-serious, half-joking tone, whispered, "There might be a Bigfoot around." We didn't hear or see anything else, but the possibility added an extra layer of thrill to our adventure.

Fast forward to my early twenties. My family, now expanded with the addition of my wife, embarked on a trip to Fairbanks. On our return drive, enveloped by the dark Alaskan night, an unexplained phenomenon occurred. A large, pulsating red light appeared in the sky. It hovered eerily and moved with agility no known aircraft could. After what felt like minutes, the light performed a rapid dance in the sky and then vanished. My parents, trailing behind in another car, witnessed the same spectacle. We were left in awe, pondering the nature of what we'd seen.

However, the most compelling of all these tales came from my wife. Late one night, she was driving home after visiting my parents. On Eagle River loop road, her headlights caught a figure. This wasn't any ordinary wildlife which we're accustomed to in Alaska. It stood upright, measuring over seven feet tall. Dark, thick fur covered its body. Its eyes, a deep shade of amber, seemed to glow, reflecting the car lights. The facial features were pronounced – a broad nose, large eyes, and unexpectedly, sharp, distinct teeth. For a few heartbeats, it looked directly at her, making a deep grunting sound before it turned and vanished into the woods.

The encounter had a profound effect on my wife. For us, this wasn't just another wild tale anymore. It was a firsthand experience from someone we trust implicitly. We've since become more attuned to the mysteries Alaska might be hiding. Conversations at family gatherings often drift to that mysterious night, and we collectively wonder what other secrets our vast and beautiful state holds.

TWELVE
VERMONT SIGHTING

IT WAS BACK in the mid-'90s, I think around '95 and '96, when I had these experiences that just don't leave my mind. I'm fairly certain they were consecutive years. And the most memorable part was when I came face to face with the creature.

I'm not sure how much you know about hunting, but there are generally two kinds: sitting and stalking. On the day of this particular encounter, the weather screamed 'stalking' – it was wet, snowy, and so close to being a rainstorm. The kind of weather where any avid hunter would hope to catch a buck in its relaxed state. But that's not me. For me, hunting was more about the peace and quiet, an escape from the world's noise. A sort of meditation, if you will.

I had a nice spot under a blue spruce tree, where I'd sit and just soak in the silence. That day, the tree was also my shield against the heavy snow. As evening approached, I was pondering heading back, hoping to beat the darkness. That's when a buck strolled into view, about 50 yards away. I slowly raised my Remington .308 and peered through the 4x9 scope. And even though I had a clear shot, something deep down told me to hold fire. Maybe it was the thought of dragging the buck through a mile of thick woods in the dark and in that sludgy weather.

As I followed the deer with my scope, it slipped behind a tree, and that's when it happened. The moment the buck went out of view, a massive figure stepped out from the same tree's other side. Bigfoot. Sasquatch. Whatever name you know him by. We locked eyes – or more accurately, my scope did. The crosshair sat right over its right eye. And let me tell you, this thing was enormous, way beyond what any story had prepared me for.

Nearby, there's this old fence post, around four and a half feet tall, which I've seen many times before. As this creature passed it, it was evident he towered over – easily double the post's height, maybe even nine feet tall. His sheer volume was mind-boggling, almost like looking at a walking wall.

He then made a half-turn, looking directly at me. His feet, however, stayed rooted in the direction the deer had gone. It was a tense moment, his gaze against the steady aim of my rifle. My mind raced with thoughts, primarily, "If this creature charges, I'm taking the shot." I recall whispering, "Don't do it Buddy. Don't do it," praying he'd understand. And as if he did, he slowly turned away and followed the path of the deer, leaving me in a mix of awe and relief.

THIRTEEN
WASHINGTON STATE SIGHTING

BACK IN JANUARY 2020, I was working a seasonal job for the Washington Department of Fish and Wildlife, primarily handling stream surveys to keep tabs on the local coho salmon population. For those unfamiliar, this involved hiking down various streams, decked out in cumbersome waders, to assess the salmon count - both alive and dead, as well as locating their egg nests. These streams, interestingly, flow directly into the Columbia River.

On that particular chilly morning, my task was to survey the "upper mill creek," a stretch farther upstream than we typically covered on Mill Creek. Getting there wasn't straightforward. My partner would usually drop me off at a starting point accessible only via Weyerhaeuser logging roads, then park our truck further downstream, marking the survey endpoint.

After being dropped off, I had about a half-mile hike on a road that had long been decommissioned. The road was punctuated with large boulders meant to deter any vehicle access. Past these obstructions, I would take a steep downhill turn, entering the forest to reach the creek below.

As I was ambling up this unused road, headphones in, lost in thought, I was nearing the point where my descent into the dense forest would begin. And that's when I saw it - a figure so out of place, it felt like my brain couldn't process it immediately. The figure was right where I was supposed to get off the main trail, almost as if it knew where I was headed.

The creature detected me first. It's alarming to think I could have possibly walked right up to it if it had stayed still. But it didn't. As I noticed it, the figure dashed uphill, its top clearing the height of the young trees in that zone. Those trees, I knew from past visits, were a tad over five feet, making the creature substantially taller. The area it dashed through had been clear cut years before and replanted.

When I revisited the area a year later, I discovered a game trail exactly where the creature had sprinted, suggesting it might have used this path frequently.

Watching it move was almost surreal. Its motions were fluid, silent, and swift - kind of like how a ninja in movies might run. The eeriest part? Even with the sunlight filtering through the trees, its jet-black form seemed to absorb every ray, casting no reflection. Its head was conical, unlike any creature I've studied or come across in my years of studying evolutionary biology. As it sprinted to the left, I only got a view of the side and back of its head, missing any facial details.

To say I was shaken would be an understatement. There I was, alone in the woods, about to embark on a survey that would last hours. Paranoia clouded my thoughts. What if it returned? Could it possibly communicate to others of its kind about my presence? For the entire duration of my survey that day, I was constantly looking over my shoulder, every rustle of leaves making my heart skip a beat.

FOURTEEN
ARKANSAS SIGHTING

IN NOVEMBER OF 1988, I lived in Arkansas. One day I rode my dirt bike down to the Twin Creek Mine. I was 14 years old, and I had ridden my dirt bike to the area near the Twin Creek River for years. Along the river stood three old piers that once supported a bridge in the 20s or 30s. One day I was standing by the edge of the water, and I was just watching large branches drift downstream. I was wondering where branches that size came from. Right about that time I heard what sounded like dogs chasing after something across the river.

I looked across the water and I caught sight of a dark, hairy creature running on two legs. It looked like a human, except it was extremely huge, probably close to eight feet tall. The large figure leaped over a dead tree log like it was nothing. The dogs were trailing it and were in hot pursuit. Once the dogs jumped over the dead logs, I lost sight of them, but I could still hear them chasing after that creature. I heard the lead dog let out a loud yelp, like something had hit it with something big and heavy. The second dog quickly turned and ran back, retracing its steps and leapt back over the log. I stood there for a few minutes, but the first dog never returned, and I never heard it make another sound. I could only imagine that whatever it was chasing turned and "eliminated" the dog.

I was terrified, knowing that I witnessed something most likely kill a dog. I didn't want to be there anymore. I didn't know what that big figure was and the last thing I wanted was to be a witness to any sort of crime or worse. I didn't waste any time and I turned and ran back to my motorcycle and raced all the way back home. Once I got there, I told everyone in the house what had happened. I was trying to not cry, but I had big tears in my eyes. I was shocked when no one believed me and to make it worse, they all started to laugh at me. I felt so betrayed by my family I turned and walked off. I know what I saw, despite their skepticism, I have always known it to be the truth. It was neither human nor a bear that hurt the dog. It was Bigfoot. It took a long time before I ever went back there, but evidently, I went back to the location. I never witnessed or heard anything like it again. Shortly after the incident with the dogs, The Old Bridge Road was closed off.

The following year, in the summer months, I had a second encounter. I was out with my friend Rick. We were cruising around and had gone for a drive along the town's main drag. When we got bored, we decided to go over to Rick's house. Rick's parents' house was at the other end of town from where I lived. They lived near an abandoned hospital on the ridge. They were grilling in the back, so we walked around the side of the house and came through the side gate. As we entered the backyard, we saw his family sitting on the patio in complete silence. We started laughing, they looked so bizarre. Rick asked what was going on and his dad told us to listen carefully.

We weren't expecting anything like this, but there suddenly was a loud, guttural roar that split pierced the air. It sounded something like a four-wheel-drive truck skidding on a highway. The strange roar repeated itself a few more times. It sounded like it was off in the woods near the old hospital. Without batting an eye, Rick and I ran inside his house and grabbed our .22 rifles and hopped into his truck. We were heading off in the direction of the hospital to see what we could find.

When we got there, we sat in the truck and rolled down the windows. We listened and heard another growl. At the same time the growl let loose, I noticed a flock of birds taking flight from deeper in the woods. It was like something spooked them and they all took flight at the same time. There were hundreds of birds flying around. We could hear over by the abandoned hospital, the sounds of snapping branches, big branches, and the clatter of rocks shifting on the creek bed. We started to get a bad feeling about this situation, so we left quickly and went back to Rick's house.

The next day, curiosity got the better of us, and we returned to the area. We walked along the creek. We stumbled upon a footprint that was huge. It was far larger than any adult man. It appears a huge barefoot creature had left its tracks in the mud. We looked around for something else. That's when I noticed that under the bridge there were a lot of branches and leaves that had been gathered. They were slightly woven together and pressed down. They almost looked like they were making a nest for something large.

Rick and I walked down closer to the "nest". I found several bone piles scattered around and under the bridge. It looked like something had been living there and eating wild animals, then throwing the bones aside. I knew no one would believe us, so we didn't tell the sheriff or our parents since all the bones looked like they were animal bones.

FIFTEEN
PENNSYLVANIA SIGHTING

WHEN I WAS fourteen years old, I went out into the woods behind my house to pick some berries and collect some acorns for a school project I was working on. It was an end of the year project, and it counted as a large part of my final grade. I hadn't done too well in school that year and I remember my teacher telling me that how well I did with and how much effort I put into my final project would determine whether I had to go to summer school to make up the class or not. I wanted more than anything to be spared the embarrassment having to go to summer school brought to someone my age back in the early nineties. I went to a good school in a small town, but in a good neighborhood and most of the kids there cared about academics. I had taken too many days off and didn't pay attention when I was there. I knew that summer school meant death to any chance of popularity the next year, when I went into high school, because it would have meant my parents would have grounded me all summer and I would've missed everything happening socially with my peers and other kids in my school. It was a big deal and I thought of the perfect project and took to the woods to collect everything I was going to need beyond what my mother had already purchased for me.

As soon as I got home from school I did my homework, had a snack, did my chores, ate dinner, and then told my mom I was going to collect some things from the woods and that I would be back as soon as I was done. It was nothing new for me to be out in those woods, the ones that surrounded my house and basically the entire town, after dark. It was a safe neighborhood and with about only ten houses on the street, and those of us that lived there being isolated from everyone and everything else in town because of the woods that surrounded our community, none of us ever worried about anything happening to me out there. There wasn't this whole need for things like "stranger danger" or "the buddy system" in my neighborhood. Plus, it was a different time. I grabbed a small basket and had an empty backpack on. I planned on getting everything I needed that night so that I had more time to hang out with my friends after school going forward. I had another two weeks to complete the project and started early so that it wouldn't become a burden to my social life. I was a fifteen-year-old girl with bigger priorities than schoolwork. I remember feeling weird from the minute I walked out of my house. It was like something was watching me. Not only that but I kept getting the chills despite the mildness of the night. Even with the sundown, it was warm. It was almost like there was some sort of electric charge to the air. I didn't recognize it for what it was at the time. The energy was off but all it felt like to me was that I was coming down with something. I didn't know anything about energy and all that back then.

I felt like something was watching me and kept looking all around to see if I could see someone. My older brothers knew I was out there and what I was doing but it was highly unlikely they would have wasted their time following me into the woods just to get a cheap scare out of me. They were usually nice to me, but someone was out there with me, I just hadn't spotted them yet. I looked all around on the ground with my flashlight. The things I was looking for were very easy to find if you knew where to look, even in the dark, and I knew those woods like the back of my hand. I had grown up in them, picnicking with my mom and camping out with my dad and then as I got older, with my friends. It wasn't unusual for me to run into some of my friends out there either because we would all always be out there in those woods doing one thing or another and with the way I was feeling at that time, I was really hoping that one of them was out there and that they would jump out and yell "gotcha!" at any given moment. However, I was out there for about fifteen minutes, and I still felt like someone was not only watching me but following me too. I had wandered around for a little bit, looking for the perfect specimens that I needed for the project and had been all over the woods at that point. The fact that I still felt stalked and watched meant that whoever it was, they were following me wherever I went.

Finally, the feeling became so intense I stopped, shined my flashlight all around and when I didn't see anything I yelled for whoever was out there to show themselves. Once I did that, I guess I became more alert because I kept hearing rustling in the trees above me where I hadn't heard anything before but again, every time I would shine my light up there and look, I didn't see anything. Finally, I decided to continue gathering the things I could get off the ground and to worry about the berries the next day when it was light out. I would go out as soon as I got home from school, before I did anything else, to avoid the fear I was feeling right then. It was incredibly uncomfortable because I had never felt anything but peace and right at home out there. The woods went on for miles and miles, and in fact I still don't know how far and wide they stretched but I know it was far. I grabbed what I could and turned around to head back to my house. I also went into my backpack and grabbed out my whistle. It was highly doubtful that anyone would hear me blowing into it where I was because I was daily deep into the woods by that point, but I always kept it on me in case I ran into a bear or some other wild, predatory animal out there. When I stopped to go into my backpack, I heard a loud thump coming from somewhere off to the side of me, about fifty yards over to my left. I jumped because it was so loud in the otherwise quiet forest. I immediately started to look around and I was immediately terrified. Something was out there with me and there was no denying it at that point. I called out again and got no reply. I heard a loud gurgling noise that sounded like it was coming from an animal. It didn't sound human, and it wasn't anything I had ever heard before in all the years I had been out in those woods. I knew it was an animal and I thought for sure I was in trouble. I zipped up my backpack, slung it back over my left shoulder and started walking as fast as I could, making my way back home. I had the whistle around my neck at that point and was just waiting for the opportunity to use it.

I heard what sounded like something very large

running very quickly behind me and then I saw rustling in the bushes over where I had just heard the strange noises. Something else had just jumped out of the trees and ran over to whatever was already on the ground, over to the side of me. I didn't see anything at first but when I shined my flashlight over in that area, four little red dots reflected off the light and just seemed to be floating there, in the middle of the tall brush and in between the trees. I stopped short and stared, trying to see what the hell was out there. I knew there were no red eyed creatures out there, at least as far as what I had been taught anyway. The more I looked, the more the dots came into focus, and I realized it was two sets of eyes. I gasped and then I immediately heard the gurgling noises again. Then a growl. I started to back away as two giant, white masses came ambling out of the brush. Each creature stood at around ten or eleven feet tall, with one of them being at least a foot shorter than the other one. I thought of polar bears immediately. It wasn't that I thought there were polar bears out there with me in the middle of a forest in northeastern Pennsylvania, but that's what they immediately reminded me of anyway. I just stared at them. Their arms were extremely long, and they had giant hands that looked more like human hands than an animal's paws. The fingers were gnarly and crooked but long and chubby. Everything about these creatures was extra. They were extra tall, extra wide, extra creepy. They just stared back at me.

The creatures were covered in white fur and had bright red eyes. I could see them very well, despite having aimed my flashlight at the ground by that point. They stuck out like a sore thumb amidst the darkness of the night and the foliage surrounding them. It's like they were just as confused as I was, or so it seemed. They kept looking from one another back to me as I stood there and watched, unable to move at all. In the middle of their bellies there was a hairless patch that took up most of the stomach itself. It wasn't exactly beige or anything, but it was a darker colored white, if that makes sense. I can still see the color to this day but haven't seen anything like it that I can really compare it too here. The tips of their fingernails and their fingernails themselves were black but not like they were dirty, it's just what color they were. They had little patches of black fur where eyebrows would be on human beings as well. Other than that, they were the purest, deepest color of white I had ever seen in my life and that's still true today. They started to look like they were agitated, and they were growling among one another. It wasn't necessarily that they were growling at me, but they were unhappy with my presence. I don't know if they were somehow tele-pathically conveying that to me if I was just reading their energy and didn't know it at the time or if I was just being paranoid and they weren't upset at all. Maybe they were just curious, but I wasn't taking any chances. I put my hand to my neck, grabbed my whistle and blew into it as hard as I could, several times. It dropped back down to my neck as the creatures both jumped very high into the air, turned, and took off running into the wilderness around us. I'll never forget how high they jumped when I scared them with that whistle. For as large and massive as they were, it should have been impossible for them to have jumped that high, and they did it in perfect unison to one another. I often look back on that specific memory and wonder if they had levitated and I just hadn't noticed because I didn't know what that was at the time. I knew nothing about bigfoot, cryptids, or anything like that. I wasn't even allowed to watch scary movies or television shows back then.

As soon as they were out of sight I ran as fast as I could to my house. I told my dad what I had seen but he told me I had to have been mistaken and my mother told me to stop making excuses for why I hadn't gotten everything I needed for the project. She then insisted on accompanying me the next day, which was fine with me after what I had just witnessed. I never encountered those creatures again but as I got older, I thought about the encounter a lot and I've done a lot of research throughout the years. In Pennsylvania specifically there are numerous encounters of what people call white bigfoot. It's an albino version of everyone's favorite cryptid, I guess. It didn't traumatize me or dissuade me from going into the woods alone, even at night, except for the first six months or so after it happened. I still think about it often and wonder what would've happened if I hadn't blown that whistle.

SIXTEEN
COLORADO SIGHTING

HAVING SPENT a good chunk of my life in the heart of Colorado, the wild outdoors was my second home. There's an allure to the state that's indescribable; perhaps it's the vastness of the forests or the ruggedness of the mountains. While most sought comfort in metropolitan city lights, I found solace among the dense woods, babbling brooks, and the thrill of the unknown. This was probably fueled by my insatiable curiosity about nature. The documentaries weren't just entertainment, they were lessons that fueled my interest and deepened my bond with the environment.

My love for adventure was complemented by Sarah, my then-girlfriend. Together, we tackled numerous trails and explored forgotten terrains. 2019 was no different. Our expedition that summer led us to a secluded camping site off Forest Rd 316, nestled between Mancos and Durango. It's a picturesque spot up in the elevation, untouched by the chaos of the world, a perfect place to disconnect.

After spending the day marvelling at the archaeological wonders of Mesa Verde, our exhausted bodies yearned for rest. Setting up camp as the sun dipped below the horizon, we got our little haven ready. As night fell, the sounds of the forest filled the void, chirping crickets, the occasional distant howl, and the wind rustling through the trees. While Sarah opted to count stars, I succumbed to my fatigue, wrapped in the cocoon of our tent.

However, our retreat was short-lived. A sudden, sharp nudge from Sarah jolted me from my slumber. Eyes wide with concern, she whispered, urging me to listen. Amidst the regular forest noises, a distinct, unfamiliar guttural sound filled the air, growing louder, closer. Its resonance was unlike any wildlife call I had ever studied.

As it drew nearer, its sheer magnitude became palpable. It knocked over a pan we had carelessly left outside, its clang echoing in the night. Panic took over Sarah, and without a second thought, she sprinted to the perceived safety of our nearby truck. But for some inexplicable reason, curiosity or sheer shock, I remained. I felt dwarfed, imagining the creature's silhouette, its breathing heavy and intense.

Frozen in place, a flurry of emotions overwhelmed me. The chilling noises it emitted were unlike anything I'd ever heard, challenging everything I knew about the natural world. Fear, wonder, regret, and curiosity mixed in a tumultuous emotional cocktail.

After what felt like hours, the creature's presence began to wane, its steps growing fainter. The absence of the moon that night was both a curse and a blessing, shielding me from its visual identity but also feeding my imagination.

Sarah and I have since parted ways, but our shared experience that night continues to bind us. We often revisit it, trying to piece together the mystery. While I've had multiple strange sightings over the years, this particular encounter stands out, emphasizing the vastness of the unknown. The incident left me with more questions than answers. Why are such occurrences so easily dismissed by society? Why does the modern world choose ignorance over exploration? It seems the answers are as elusive as the creature itself.

SEVENTEEN
OKLAHOMA SIGHTING

HAVING SPENT my formative years in Northern Oklahoma, I've had my fair share of adventures and experiences. My grandfather's sprawling property sat near the Cow Creek watersheds, approximately 30 minutes from Ponca and a short 15-minute ride from both Pawnee and Red Rock. The vastness of Lake McMurty was just a half-hour drive in the opposite direction.

Back in the day, my grandfather's property spanned a massive 500 acres, equivalent to a square mile. Over time, though, he downsized to a more manageable 125 acres, known locally as a "Quarter." The property wasn't just open land; it boasted two sizable ponds and a pristine, ever-flowing natural spring that streamed toward the watershed. It was a sanctuary for many animals, as hunting was strictly prohibited. Grandpa had acquired this land back in the early '40s and, over the years, bred various livestock and animals, which he eventually sold at the Stillwater Auctions. However, by the early '80s, he decided to sell the property.

I was ten during my first encounter. While fishing at a neighbor's pond with my family, my brother and I, unimpressed with our luck, decided to hunt for ring necks and horned toads. Distracted by our search on the ground, my brother suddenly exclaimed about seeing a tree fall. Intrigued, we raced over to the spot. But what we saw wasn't just a fallen tree; it was a creature resembling Bigfoot, fleeing in the opposite direction. We scrambled back in panic to where our stepdad was fishing. Though we were convinced of what we'd seen, he brushed it off as our wild imagination and continued fishing, leaving us nervously watching the woods from the safety of our pickup.

The second and third encounters were intertwined, occurring when I was 13. Armed with a shotgun, my friend Charles and I were on a quail hunt on my grandpa's property. As we traversed deeper into the woods, we stumbled upon a clearing. Excitedly, I shot down a bird that flew out, which landed in a thick bush. Upon inspection, Charles commented about a strong, foul smell emanating from the thicket, jokingly attributing it to my downed bird. We decided to head back as we neared the watershed area boundary.

On our return, we felt an eerie sensation of being watched and followed. The heavy footsteps behind us were initially dismissed as maybe a wandering cow, but the synchronized pace of the unknown entity left us unnerved. We bolted out of the woods into an open field, only to witness a towering Bigfoot-like creature emerge from the forest, observing us from behind large trees. The sheer size and appearance of the creature left us petrified.

Regaining our senses, we sprinted to my grandpa's house. In our distraught state, we narrated our ordeal to my family. My grandmother, ever the skeptic, challenged us to lead her to the creature. Reluctantly, and armed with just frog gigs, we retraced our steps. The creature made another appearance, lurking behind a large cedar tree. Standing roughly 15 feet away, I could make out its matted, clay-red hair, wide nose, and dark, brown eyes. The color seemed a mix of brown with specks of red clay, giving it a uniquely rustic appearance.

We locked eyes with the creature for what felt like hours before finally deciding to retreat. The next day, with a group including my stepdad, we found tracks corresponding to our mysterious entity. While he acknowledged that something had trailed us, he remained non-committal about it being Bigfoot. But those encounters left an indelible mark on my memory, forever changing my perception of the wild and the unknown.

EIGHTEEN
MONTANA SIGHTING

GROWING UP, my life was packed with outdoor adventures. From family camping and fishing trips in the Little Belt mountains to my youthful hunting days, the wilderness and I have always been thick as thieves. I spent my twenties scaling the rocky cliffs of the northwest with my close pal, Todd. Rock climbing was an adrenaline-packed passion of ours, and together we experienced some of the best views nature had to offer.

In the last decade and a half, my relationship with nature has taken a more relaxed turn. As a fly fishing guide, not only do I enjoy the serene environments, but I also get to interact with many people, sharing stories and experiences. For a change of pace and a dose of adrenaline, I also dive into dirt biking, tearing through trails and often finding myself lost in the vast wilderness.

But here's where it gets interesting. On my 25-acre

property where my cabin sits, some seriously weird stuff goes down. While I've never actually spotted a sasquatch, I've heard some distinct sounds – close-range whoops and what sounded like whistling directed at my wife. But that's not all. Curiously placed marbles appear out of nowhere, and sticks, for some reason, seem to balance themselves on a far-off property marker. Every time I remove them, they reappear, as if placed deliberately. On a couple of occasions, I've even heard what sounds like children giggling in the vicinity. Oddly enough, these events mostly occur during the fall.

Recently, after tuning into episode 884, a conversation between you and Taylor got me thinking. The topic was the power of thought and how sometimes, we might "will" things into existence. This resonated deeply with an experience I had last November. I'll lay out the full story, no omissions.

I remember the day clearly. After a satisfying dirt biking session, I was driving home via the scenic back roads. Traversing through La Hood canyon by the Jefferson river, the dim twilight was settling in. I thought to myself, "Man, if I ever have a sasquatch encounter, I hope it's from the safety of this truck." Just then, my headlights caught something on the left – at first glance, it seemed like deer fur. But as I approached, it became clear: four upright, human-like figures. My immediate reaction was, "Oh, just some hunters in matching camo."

But as I drove past and glanced in my rearview mirror, something seemed off. One of them raised its arms, revealing an unnaturally long span. Their physique resembled tall, athletic basketball players. Thinking they might be stranded, I decided to double back to offer assistance.

By the time I returned to the spot, they were nowhere in sight. I drove as far as the Lewis and Clark Caverns, thinking there was no way they could've walked so fast. On my way back, I spotted them again, this time on the railroad tracks by the Jefferson River. When I yelled out an offer for help, their reaction was bizarre. They seemed to glide rather than run along the tracks and, after my second shout, they ducked down, peeking over occasionally. The air was thick with unease, prompting me to hit the road ASAP.

Now, I can't say with absolute certainty what I witnessed that day. But after your discussion on willing things into reality, I can't help but wonder – did I inadvertently summon these mysterious figures?

NINETEEN
ALASKA SIGHTING

WHEN MY FRIEND'S father passed away, he was overwhelmed by grief. Understanding how challenging it was for him to be alone, I thought some fresh air and a change of scenery might help him cope. I suggested we take a drive up the scenic Alaska highway, a route he had always cherished. It was a spontaneous decision, and as a result, our journey began later in the day. Before we realized, the darkness of night had already set in, and we were navigating the highway with caution. The 80km stretch before reaching Fort Nelson was especially notorious for its unexpected wildlife encounters, including moose, bears, and other animals.

As the clock struck 1:30am, our peaceful drive was interrupted. A visibly distressed large buck burst onto the road, its movements erratic, signaling alarm. Given the steep embankments on either side of the road, we pulled over, fearing that other animals might follow and pose a danger.

My friend stepped out to take a brief break and stretch his legs, while I remained near the car, captivated by the deer's attempts to clamber up the embankment. Suddenly, an alarming crash echoed in the night, followed by a silence so deep it was almost tangible. That's when I saw it.

Emerging from the shadowy veil of the night were two intensely glowing, whitish-silver eyes. These weren't just any eyes; they seemed almost unnaturally large and had an innate luminosity as if harboring their own light source. The dim light barely revealed the creature's features, but those radiant eyes offered a glimpse. The pupils were pronounced, set in a wide, flat face that hinted at its potential size. The creature's nose was broad and flattened, adding to its already peculiar face. Its head, appearing disproportionally large, was round, and atop it seemed to be tufts of shaggy, coarse hair that rustled gently with the breeze.

Under those luminous eyes, I could faintly discern high cheekbones and what appeared to be a small, downturned mouth. It seemed to have a powerful jawline, suggesting immense strength. The creature's silhouette hinted at broad shoulders and a muscular build, making it evident that it was something not to be trifled with.

I yelled to my friend, hoping to draw his attention to this surreal sight. Perhaps due to his emotional state or sheer exhaustion, he gave it a cursory glance and insisted we leave immediately, fearing our safety might be compromised.

Later, piecing together the night's events, I couldn't shake off the feeling that we had witnessed a Sasquatch. I recalled a previous encounter in a similar region, making the theory seem even more plausible. The terrain was challenging, yet this being held its ground with an ease that defied logic. The more I thought about it, the more I became convinced that the creature, possibly with others of its kind, was hunting the deer. The eeriness of the sudden silence after the deer's struggle was a chilling reminder of nature's raw, unpredictable side.

TWENTY
FLORIDA SIGHTING

LATE OCTOBER 1999 remains one of the most unforgettable months for me after we had recently migrated to Sebring, Florida from Canada. The drastic change from Canada's cool climate to Florida's humidity was just one of the many adjustments we had to make. We were temporarily renting a house in a secluded gated community, which, despite its apparent safety, was bordered by mysterious, swampy terrains.

As a teenager, nights became especially daunting since my mother often worked night shifts at a nearby hospital. Thus, my younger brother and I found ourselves fending for each other during these times. To make matters more challenging, we were on a strict budget, so luxuries like central air conditioning were off-limits. On one such stifling night, in a bid to battle the relentless heat, I remember propping open my bedroom window and placing a small oscillating fan on the sill, hoping for a semblance of coolness.

A sudden disturbance interrupted my restless sleep that night. The distressed meows of my cat echoed in the silent night. Glancing out, my eyes traced his frantic run from the back of our yard. Instinct kicked in, and without a second thought, I bolted outside, managing to retrieve him. As I rushed back inside, a chilling realization hit me - something had scared my usually fearless cat.

However, the terror had only just begun. As soon as I re-entered my room, a foul, almost nauseating odor filled the air. The unsettling mix of sweaty body odor with the pungency of rotten eggs made my stomach churn. Swallowing my apprehension, I hesitantly peeked outside, unprepared for the sight that awaited me.

Looming over our lawn was an enormous creature, its features barely discernible in the dim light. It bore a striking resemblance to a gorilla but with an all-black coat and a distinctly smoother head. The sheer size of it was staggering, with muscular arms that seemed to rest heavily on the ground. But what truly shook me was its peculiar behavior. It sat motionless for a moment, then began to move in an inexplicable manner, swaying its arms and shifting its broad shoulders, all while its legs remained firmly anchored to the ground.

As fear gripped me, I wrestled with the idea of calling

my mom. Was I hallucinating? But another peek confirmed its ominous presence. Desperate for a better, clearer view, I dashed to the back patio doors. However, to my astonishment, the creature had vanished without a trace. My frantic searches from other windows yielded nothing. As suddenly as it had appeared, the creature — and the accompanying stench — had dissipated.

That incident cast a long shadow over my time in Sebring. Even though I never encountered the creature again, an unsettling feeling of being constantly watched often overcame me, especially during solitary walks in the neighborhood. The fetid smell that I associated with the creature would sometimes waft in during hikes on local community trails.

Years later, a serendipitous encounter with a documentary on the Florida Skunk Ape made everything fall into place. The accounts shared on the show were eerily reminiscent of my own experience. With a shiver down my spine, I realized that I had likely come face-to-face with the legendary Skunk Ape, a creature deeply woven into Florida's folklore.

TWENTY-ONE
ARIZONA SIGHTING

ALRIGHT, let me walk you through a strange encounter my brother and I had on a warm August night. Living close to the Sonoran desert, we know that the daytime heat can be brutal. So, wanting to explore and hopefully see some nocturnal wildlife, we decided to set out once the sun had set.

A friend had recently told my brother about an app called "Rando naughting". It sounds a bit out there, but it basically generates random coordinates for you to go to. You're supposed to think of something you want to find or manifest, and then it guides you to a location that supposedly the universe wouldn't have otherwise set you on - disrupting the natural order of things, as some enthusiasts describe it.

It was a bit past 10:30 pm, and despite being night-time, it was still sweltering at around 101 degrees. With the app downloaded and our coordinates set, we headed out. We eventually reached a trailhead, and the moment we stepped out, there was this uneasy feeling in the pit of our stomachs. It felt like we were being watched. The uneasiness was so palpable that my brother and I exchanged nervous glances, but neither of us voiced our discomfort.

We tried shaking off the feeling and proceeded further into the wash and then up the bank. By this point, our car was quite a distance away, but we couldn't shake off the sensation of being watched. My brother suddenly whipped around, indicating towards our jeep, and said, "There's someone there. Do you see that?" Looking over, I saw a figure hovering around our car. It was tall - definitely taller than my 6-foot-tall brother. Both of us, taken aback, were trying to come up with logical conclusions. Perhaps a wandering horse? Or maybe a biker who happened to be out unusually late?

Just as we were brainstorming, my brother sharply grabbed my arm and pointed to a bush not too far from our vehicle. What we saw made our blood run cold. A set of eyes - unmistakably eyes because they blinked several times - was visible just over the top of the bush. They had a distinct soft blue glow, and from the way they moved, it seemed like the creature was trying to avoid our flashlight. It then went still, peering over the bush as if it was standing upright.

Panic took over, and we started running towards the eyes, shouting, partly out of fear and partly in a futile attempt to scare the creature off. But by the time we reached the location, there was no sign of the entity. Standing next to that bush, it hit us - the bush itself was over 6 1/2 feet tall. That meant the creature would have had to be around 7-8 feet tall. We scoured the surrounding area, searching for footprints or any other signs, but there was nothing.

Recounting the event, my brother and I were both baffled. Those blue eyes were nothing like we'd ever seen. They weren't those of an owl; we know owls. And cougars? Their eyes glow greenish-white, plus they can't stand that tall. The closest thing we could relate it to was perhaps a Sasquatch, given that we were in a large preserve with ample hiding spots.

I later visited the site with my dad, and even without knowing our previous experience, he immediately felt uneasy and suggested we leave. Ever since, I've avoided returning to that place at night. I can't get over that strange energy we felt and the way those eyes looked at us. It was beyond bizarre!

———

CONTINUE WITH
I SAW BIGFOOT, BOOK 4

ABOUT THE AUTHOR

Ethan Hayes grew up in Oklahoma and moved to Texas when he attended Texas A&M. Upon graduation he was hired by Texas Parks and Wildlife and remained there until he retired twenty-two years later. He currently lives in southeast Texas with his wife and two dogs. When he's not spending time enjoying the outdoors and writing, he sips a cold beer on his front porch while listening to Bluegrass music.

———

Send in your encounter story:
encountersbigfoot@gmail.com

ALSO BY ETHAN HAYES

ALSO BY FREE REIGN PUBLISHING